COSMO'S GREAT ADVENTURES

The Case of the
Whatever
Blues

Toot-toot

Cosmo

Written by Suzanne Kline • Illustrated by Daryl Slaton

Published by
HAPPY CREEK PRESS, INC.
Asheville, NC

This book is dedicated to my creative and powerful son, Gary, and to my four grandsons -- Tyler, Devin, Keegan and Colin - who taught me the power of living and creating joy in each and every moment.

"This world is but a canvas to our imaginations."
Henry David Thoreau

"People are just as happy as they make up their minds to be."
Abraham Lincoln

Copyright © 2009 by Suzanne Kline and Daryl Slaton

For information contact
Happy Creek Press, Inc. c/o Patricia Adamson at P.O. Box 1638,
Weaverville, N.C. 28787-1638. • Phone: 828-645-5885.

Cosmo Adventure series books are happily published and distributed by Happy Creek Press, Inc.
P.O. Box 1638, Weaverville, N.C. 28787-1638.
www.happycreekpress.com

Contact Cosmo at
www.cosmosgreatadventures.com

ISBN 13: 978-0-9823702-0-9
ISBN 10: 0-9823702-0-2

1st Printing, May 2009
Printed in China by Imago

Library of Congress Control Number: 2009923704

Book Design and Illustrations created by: Daryl Slaton, Biltmore Lake, N.C. *www.octoberrocket.com*
Cosmo photography by: Suzanne Kline, Weaverville, N.C.
Happily Edited by: Rev. Dr. John B. Waterhouse, *www.CSLAsheville.org*
and Liisa Sullivan, *www.writeawayplus.com*

COSMO'S GREAT ADVENTURES

The Case of the Whatever Blues

LIVE HAPPY!

Cosmo Approved!

HAPPY CREEK PRESS, INC.

just imagine...

One morning...

Yawn!

Cosmo's Room

Cosmo woke up in the usual way, on an ordinary day, just like all the other dogs...

Cosmo always woke up happy, but today was a different kind of day!

Cosmo looked into the mirror and yawned as his sleepy,
brown eyes peered back at him.

He noticed that the neighborhood seemed unusually quiet.
Dogs weren't barking...
The rooster wasn't crowing at the early morning dawn...
and most strangely the birds weren't singing their happy songs...

Cosmo shrugged and proclaimed his morning saying,
"Today is a *happy day*!!"

He then brushed his teeth, washed his face, and smiled a big smile.

Downstairs he went. Again, Cosmo noticed how very quiet
the neighborhood was this morning…
"Something feels different," thought Cosmo!

The family was up and everyone seemed to be in a bad mood…
Mom was watching television and the news reported bad
things were happening. Mom agreed that the world was very
unhappy today!

"Whatever," said Mom as she shrugged and repeated unhappily,
"WHATEVER!"

Meanwhile, on the Internet, Cosmo decided to check out the news for himself. Even the Internet was reporting how unhappy the world was today! The Internet headlines reported that the president was saying, "Whatever, whatever today!"

As Cosmo read the headlines, he just smiled and thought to himself, "If I was president, I would declare everyday is a happy day!"

Just then, Squirrely Shirley peered in through the window and asked, "Oh, Cosmo, you are a silly little dog! Don't you know that everyone's not always happy?"

Cosmo just laughed because he knew everyday was a happy day. He then ran outside to play with Squirrely Shirley and coaxed, "Come on, Shirley, let's play! It is a beautiful, happy day!"

Shirley sneered back at Cosmo, "Oh, whatever Cosmo! I have more important things to take care of today! And, all you want to do is play. WHATEVER!"

Cosmo jumped up and down and laughed as he watched Squirrely Shirley run off in a huff. Shirley repeated back, "Whatever, Cosmo! You are way too happy for me!"

Cosmo looked around his backyard and saw that even the butterflies and dragonflies were uttering, "Whatever, whatever! It's a whatever kind of day!" And the birds were chirping, **"Whatever! Whatever!"**

At that very moment, Cosmo shouted out, "Come on everyone! Don't you know we create our world?"

"Look around you!" said Cosmo. "The sun is shining, there are fluffy white clouds in the sky… and our world is a beautiful place to play and have fun!"

"Let's all play!"

"Whatever! Whatever!" shouted everyone to Cosmo.

At this moment, Cosmo knew that it was up to him. He focused on his happiness inside and decided right then and there to make it his mission to help everyone snap out of the "Whatever Blues!"

Cosmo said, "I will claim this day as happy and live my own idea of a happy day! I know I can!"

Just then, Squirrely Shirley appeared from around the tree and asked, "Oh, Cosmo! That's just like you! How are you, a little scruffy dog, going to do anything? You are stuck in this yard just like everyone else! Shirley snarled, "Whatever, Cosmo!"

"Whatever!"

"NO!" exclaimed Cosmo! "We all have the choice and power within us to be anything we want to be!"

Cosmo proclaimed,

"One of the most important parts of me is my imagination!"

"I can always imagine fun ways to be happy! I know I can be and do anything as long as I can see it in my mind … so, I'm not stuck!"

"Want to go along with me, Shirley?" asked Cosmo.
"Want to go along with me on my great adventure?"
"Sure. Whatever, Cosmo," Shirley replied in doubt!

"Close your eyes," Cosmo told Shirley. "Trust and feel it from the top of your head to the bottom of your toes! Here we go... let's go!"

It was just a moment when Shirley opened her eyes and exclaimed, "Wow, Cosmo! It really works!!!" Shirley could not believe her eyes because...

Cosmo was driving a beautiful car. He was speeding along with his ears flopping in the wind!

"Weeeeee! Now do you see, Shirley?" Cosmo howled in glee. "I see fun travels everywhere around us!" Cosmo exclaimed,

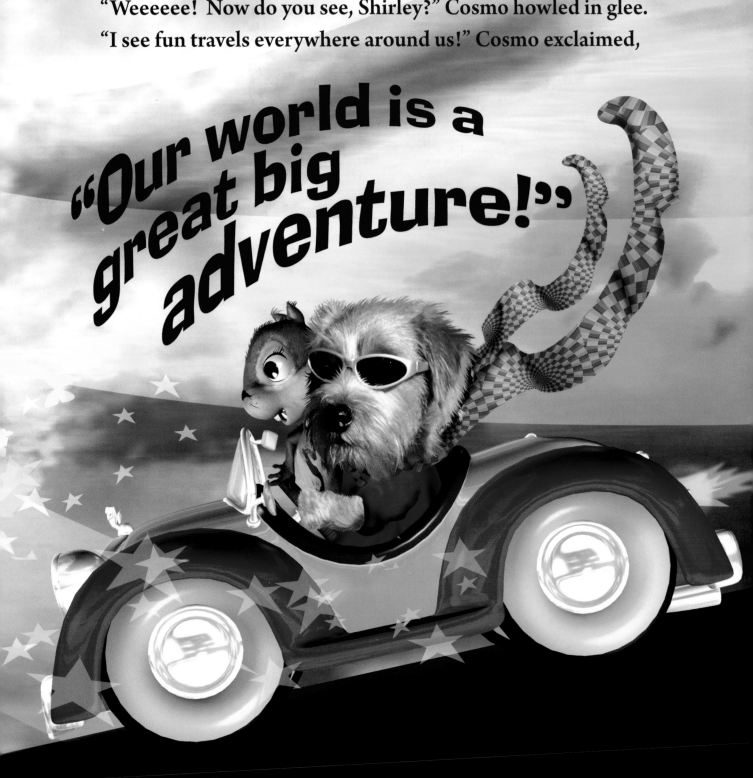

"Our world is a great big adventure!"

Cosmo and Shirley clapped in pure joy! Cosmo asked Shirley, "Have you ever imagined yourself in a place like this?"

The yard they lived in was far behind them. All they could see ahead was fun and new adventures!

Cosmo let out the happiest howl ever and said, "Anything is possible, Shirley! *We can see, believe and BE whatever we choose!*"

Cosmo and Shirley passed many other animals. They all joined in the howling laughter and watched in amazement at the sight of Cosmo and Shirley speeding by them in the shiny, new car!

"Hey, Shirley!" Cosmo howled. "Let's see everyone in the world as happy today!"

All at once, everywhere they drove, everything around them looked beautiful.

Then, in the next instant, a beautiful rainbow appeared right in front of them. Cosmo shouted, "Beauty is everywhere I look! I see joy and happiness everywhere!"

Squirrely Shirley still had a difficult time believing they were really driving down a road together. She asked Cosmo, "How did we get here? Is this real, Cosmo?"

"Of course, it's real!" Cosmo happily expressed to Shirley! "Yes we can! We just have to *think it, see it, feel it and believe it!* It's like magic!" Cosmo laughed, "All this just takes practice!"

"You believe and the magic becomes real!"

Cosmo then asked Shirley what she always wanted to be. Shirley closed her eyes and imagined it clearly…

And all at once, Shirley and Cosmo were in a pink rocket ship, flying high above the world!

Shirley exclaimed in glee, as she opened her eyes wide,
"Wow! Cosmo, I have always wanted to be an astronaut
and now I am! Weeeeee! This is fun being me!"

The world was so beautiful from the inside of a rocket ship. Shirley's dream had come true and now she was flying high above the trees! She was an astronaut piloting her own

As Shirley steered the rocket ship, Cosmo imagined a cosmic rainbow maker. It made beautiful rainbows that streamed from the rocket ship, touching everyone on the Earth. They watched as the cosmic rainbow maker spread beautiful rainbows all over the world!

In fact, the rainbows were so beautiful that Shirley named the rocket ship, "Cosmo's Cosmic Rainbow Maker!" Cosmo shouted in joy, "Beauty is everywhere!"

"Wherever I look I see joy!"

And so it went. Cosmo and Shirley spent a magical day together, flying around the world. The rainbows from the rocket ship continued to spread joy everywhere and to change the "Whatever Blues" into a happy day for everyone, everywhere!

Cosmo was thrilled. He took all of it into his heart and, at that very moment, he knew that he had found a real buddy in Shirley.

Cosmo felt his happiness expand as he thought about his new buddy, Shirley. They had so many more experiences and great adventures to share ahead!

Cosmo thought, "It sure is fun to have a true friend who I can be happy together with in this world."

Cosmo howled out loud,

"I am so happy! I know I am in a world that loves me… and happiness is my choice!"

In the blink of an eye, Cosmo and Shirley were back home again…

blink!

...safe and sound in their beautiful back yard!
But, guess what??? *Something was different...*

Now, the birds were singing and chirping a happy song!

The rooster was crowing happily all day long! The dogs were barking merrily a happy chorus of howls filled with joy! The butterflies were dancing in the golden rays of sunshine and the dragonflies were touching every flower with a happy, golden light!

Cosmo and Shirley watched as the whole garden came alive with beautiful colors...

Mom turned off the television and came out to play with Cosmo.
She was so happy.

The whole world was filled with joy, and of course, rainbows!
Everyone in the world was living as ONE HAPPY FAMILY!

Everyday is A HAPPY DAY!!!